Also by Gerald Rose

The Bag of Wind
The Bird Garden
How St Francis Tamed the Wolf
(with text by Elizabeth Rose)
Scruff
Trouble in the Ark

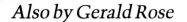

British Library Cataloguing in Publication Data
Rose, Gerald, 1935-
The fisherman and the cormorants.
I. Title
823'.914J PZ7
ISBN 0-370-31060-8

Copyright © Gerald Rose 1987
Printed in Italy for
The Bodley Head
32 Bedford Square, London WC1B 3EL
by New Interlitho, Spa, Milan
First published 1987

THE FISHERMAN AND THE CORMORANTS

Gerald Rose

The Bodley Head
London

A long time ago, a fisherman lived with his family on the banks of the River Li.

One year there had been little rain, the river was low and fish were difficult to catch. The fisherman worked hard all day, but by nightfall he had caught only one small fish. He placed the fish on the deck of his boat and headed for home.

On the far bank of the river, a cormorant sat watching the fisherman. She, too, had been fishing all day without success. She knew that if she didn't catch anything before morning, her three chicks would starve.

Flying low over the water,

the cormorant snatched
the fish from the deck of
the boat and flew back
to the nest.

Her chicks were well fed that night.

The fisherman returned to his family. When his wife discovered that he had not brought any fish for them to eat, she beat him with a bamboo cane, and his children cried, for they were tired of eating just rice and vegetables.

The next day, the fisherman worked even harder, but after many hours he had again only caught one small fish. He laid it on the deck of his boat and headed for home.

The cormorant watched him from the far bank. She had caught nothing all day, and her chicks were again very hungry. She flew towards the boat. But this time the fisherman was on the look-out…

and as the cormorant swooped to snatch the fish, he threw a net over her.

The cormorant cried out in despair, "Oh please let me go! My chicks are hungry and they will surely die, if I do not return with some fish to feed them with."

The kind-hearted fisherman took pity on the bird. He knew that his own children had rice and vegetables and they would not starve, so he gave the fish to the cormorant and let her go.

When the fisherman returned home to his family empty-handed, his wife beat him soundly with her bamboo cane and his children cried even louder than before.

The following day it rained. The river rose and the fish returned. The cormorant was able to feed her family without stealing from the fisherman, and the fisherman's children had fish again for their supper.

Many full moons rose over the river, and the fisherman had almost forgotten the incident, when there was another drought. The river dropped again, and the fish disappeared. But this year the crops had failed, too, and so the fisherman had no rice and vegetables to give his children. Each night they went to bed hungry.

One day, after fishing for many hours, the fisherman turned round and noticed three small cormorants flying towards his boat.

"There's no fish for them to steal this time," he thought ruefully.

The fisherman reached for his bamboo pole to fend off the birds, but before he could do so...

the cormorants dropped three fish at his feet.

As the fisherman stared at them in amazement, one of the cormorants said, "We are the birds you saved when we were starving, and in return for your kindness then, we will help you to feed your family until the fish return to the river. Beyond the mountain there is a deep pool full of fish, and we will bring some for your family each day."

The cormorants kept their word, and each day they brought three fish. The fisherman's children had plenty to eat, until eventually the rains came, the river rose and the fish returned.

The fisherman's children and the cormorant's children remembered the friendship. To this day, there are fishermen along the banks of the River Li who use birds rather than hooks or nets to catch fish. The cormorants are attached to the boat by a long length of twine. The birds dive for the fish, which they then deliver to the fishermen. Because cormorants are at times a little greedy, a piece of string is tied round their throats to prevent them swallowing the catch, but when enough fish have been caught, the string is removed and the birds are able to feed themselves.